I Want to Be a Cavegirl!

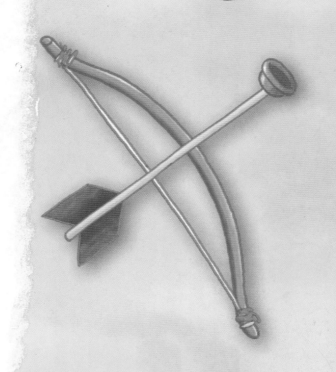

I Want to Be a Cavegirl!

Tony Ross

Andersen Press · London

The castle was crammed with chambers, staircases and interesting hidey-holes, but today the Little Princess only wanted to play in the garden shed.

Licensed by The Illuminated Film Company
Based on the LITTLE PRINCESS animation series © The Illuminated Film Company 2008.
Made under licence by Andersen Press Ltd., London
'I Want to be a Cavegirl!' episode written by Dave Ingham.
Producer Iain Harvey. Director Edward Foster.
© The Illuminated Film Company/Tony Ross 2008.
Design and layout © Andersen Press Ltd, 2008.
Printed and bound in China by Midas Printing Ltd.
10   9   8   7   6   5   4   3   2   1
British Library Cataloguing in Publication Data available.

ISBN: 978 1 84270 765 4

This book has been printed on acid-free paper

"I need a bit more here for the whiskers…" she mumbled. "And now some teeth!"

The Little Princess chalked some pointy bits onto her blackboard, then stepped back.

"Do you like my cave drawing?" Puss and Scruff looked confused.

The Little Princess hushed to a whisper.
"A long, long, longy-long time ago, even longer than mum and dad, there weren't castles to live in," she explained.
"Everyone used to live in caves."
Scruff looked sheepishly at the fierce dog on the blackboard.

"Grrrrrr!" growled the Little Princess. "I want to be a cavegirl!"
Cavegirls were much better than princesses. They got to hunt and make cave music.

Indoors, the King and Queen were just about to tuck into their royal lunch.

"Princess!" gasped the Queen.

The Little Princess scowled. "I'm not a princess any more. I'm a cavegirl."

She stomped up to the table and grabbed a sausage in her fist.

Lunch was extremely messy.

"Bu-rrp!" belched the Little Princess. "Yummy!"
The King and Queen gawped as their daughter stuffed the
sausages and mash into her mouth with her hands.

"Are you sure you can't use your knife and fork, sweetheart?"
asked the Queen.

"No!" barked the Little Princess. "Cavegirls eat like this!"

The Little Princess grinned cheekily. "Cavegirls just do what they want."

"Oh dear," sighed the Queen.

"And I've decided that I'm going to live in a cave from now on. Bye!"

The Little Princess went out hunting in the castle garden.
She took a deep breath and pulled back her bow. Boiinng!

An arrow was sent whistling up towards the sky,
then down into a bush.

The bush shook. "Ouch!"

The Little Princess squealed. "I've got something!"

"Look what you've done to Nessie!"
The General clambered awkwardly out of the bushes.

"Sorry, Nessie," grinned the Little Princess. "I'm hunting for wild animals."

"Is it fun?" asked the General. The Little Princess nodded, then handed over the bow and arrow.

"Take the weight off your wheel, Nessie," grinned the General. "I'm having a go!"

It was a cracking shot.
"I've got something!"
cried the General.

"Maybe it's a woolly mammoth," said
the Little Princess. "That's what they
call big, hairy elephants."

"Ahem!" The Maid stormed out from behind the washing line.

"S-s-sorry," stuttered the General. "I thought you were a big, hairy elephant."

"Um-bamba-lamb-a!"
chanted the Little Princess.

She started to beat on a
cardboard box, using two old
recorders as sticks.

"This cavegirl drum
is **perfect!**"

The Little Princess whacked and thwacked the
box so loudly, she didn't notice poor Puss rattling
around inside.

"Cavegirls dance a lot," she bellowed. "And they play
cave music!"

The Maid arrived to take the Princess indoors.
"It's time to have a bath," she announced. "And to get
that hair combed!"
The Little Princess shook her head. She wasn't
going anywhere.

"But it's time to come in now," argued the Maid.

"No!" cried the Little Princess. "This is my cave and I'm staying in here all night!"

The cavegirl slammed the shed door behind her.

It was time for the Maid to call in the King and Queen.

The Queen tapped gently on the shed door. "Come back to the castle, Princess."

"You can always be a cavegirl tomorrow," suggested the King.

The Little Princess flung open the door.
"I'm a cavegirl all day and all night."
The King nodded wisely. "OK, cavegirl it is then.
Sleep well, poppet."
"Cave mummy will be inside if you need her,"
added the Queen.

The garden was very dark at night-time, but the Little Princess felt cosy inside her cave. It was fun being a cavegirl, snuggled up next to Puss and Scruff.

Tu-whit-tu-whoo!

The Little Princess clicked on the light.

"That was only an owl."

Quack-quack-quack!

"That must be a duck on the pond," she whispered.

"But I might leave the light on."

The Little Princess peeped nervously out of the window.

"I thought I heard something outside," she gasped.

Cr-rack!

"I think maybe being a p-p-princess isn't all that bad," stuttered the Little Princess.

Suddenly the door started to open.

"I want Gilbert!" screamed the Little Princess. "It's a big, hairy elephant!"

The door swung open revealing…

…the Maid!

"I just thought you might be peckish, Cavegirl," she said.

"And I brought Gilbert for you."

The Little Princess reached out to cuddle her teddy.
"Thanks," she beamed. "You can call me Princess, if you like."

The Little Princess was tucked up in her castle bedroom in no time. The bed seemed to feel extra comfy tonight. "Goodnight, poppet," whispered the King.

"Are you cosy?" asked the Queen, turning down the light.
The Little Princess yawned happily and nodded.
"I like being a cavegirl in the day…

...but nothing's better than being a princess at night!"